COWGIRL DREAMS

JENNIFER OWINGS DEWEY

COWGIRL DREAMS

A Western Childhood

with drawings by the author

Boyds Mills Press

Published by Caroline House
Boyds Mills Press, Inc.
A Highlights Company
815 Church Street
Honesdale, Pennsylvania 18431
Printed in the United States of America

Publisher Cataloging-in-Publication Data
Dewey, Jennifer Owings.
Cowgirl dreams : a western childhood / Jennifer Owings Dewey.—1st ed.
[144]p. ; cm.
Foreword by Brinton Turkle.
Summary : The author's childhood memories of living on a ranch in New Mexico.
ISBN 1-56397-377-4
1. New Mexico—Juvenile biography. 2. Ranch life—West (U.S.)—Juvenile literature.
[1. New Mexico—Biography. 2. Ranch life.] I. Title.
92—dc20 [B] 1995 CIP AC
Library of Congress Catalog Card Number 94-73317

First edition, 1995
The text of this book is set in 14-point Berkeley Old Style Book.
Distributed by St. Martin's Press

10 9 8 7 6 5 4 3 2 1

*This book is dedicated to children growing up wild,
free, and informed.*

Contents

Foreword

Skies in New Mexico are bluer and broader than anywhere else I know. Red canyons furrow high mesas. Mountains stand as green sentinels until autumn, when aspen turn them gold before snow whitens them. New Mexico is harsh and beautiful. With good reason it is called "The Land of Little Rain" and "The Land of Enchantment."

Officially, three cultures are at home here: Indian, Hispanic, and Anglo—a strange category for all other people, including Africans and Asians.

I am never more enchanted than when I am standing in the sunny plaza of a Rio Grande pueblo watching summer harvest dances or winter animal dances. Christianity was introduced here three hundred years ago, but these dances are an expression of a much older religion. Visitors are welcomed at most ceremonies. Festive as these occasions are, the painted dancers in their feathers, woven kilts, colorful mantles, and silver and turquoise jewelry dance solemnly. Women shuffle barefoot, keeping close contact with the earth. Men pound the ground more briskly in their moccasins. Even little children wearing replicas of their elders' costumes take part, trying to learn the intricate steps. The unpredictable drumbeats, the rattles and bells attached to the men's legs, the chanting, and even the piñon smoke drifting from surrounding adobe chimneys make an unforgettable experience.

Several decades ago, a little Anglo girl who lived on a ranch close to San Ildefanso Pueblo often watched her Indian playmates dance. Once she was so caught up with excitement that she joined the dancers without the proper costume or heritage. No one stopped her. That little girl was Jennifer Owings.

Today Jennifer Owings Dewey enters the animal world with the same excitement and aplomb as she entered the Indian world. A raven was once part of her family. Her ecological curiosity is insatiable and has led her as far away as Antarctica. But animals of the Southwest interest her the most. Creatures such as bats, snakes, and spiders that are feared or shunned by most people intrigue and delight her. As she roams the deserts, the mesas, and the mountains of her native land, she shows these animals the respect they deserve.

This true story is about a small girl and her pig—an animal not often thought of as a pet. On the ranch where she grew up, Jennifer—with only the grudging approval of her father—adopted the runt of a litter. Farm and ranch children are ill-advised to make a pet of something that might end up on the supper table. She called her pig Jerome, the noblest name she could think of. Her story of joy and heartbreak is told with rare candor. It is the story of a remarkable young girl who loved her land with passion—and who still does.

BRINTON TURKLE

Santa Fe, New Mexico
1995

Jerome Is Born

Bill Burnham was a cowboy, and he was my hero. Bill was in his forties when I was a kid. His job was to run the ranch my father owned, a two-hundred-and-fifty-acre spread in northern New Mexico. I grew up on the ranch. It was the center of my universe until I turned fourteen.

Bill was originally from east Texas, a region of

the country he called "bleak." He said he never considered the world round until he got to New Mexico. "You have mountains here," he said. "Indians live in New Mexico, and Spanish folks, and Anglos like you and me. I like it fine here."

I was glad Bill liked it fine. If he'd have taken it into his head to leave, I might have followed. That's how much I cared about him.

I also worshiped Edna, Bill's wife. She was our cook, but she did a lot more. She ran the half-acre vegetable garden, and she managed the fruit orchard. A big part of her life was watching my two sisters and me. "Those children are spoiled and savage," my father liked to say. "See what you can do to make them human, Edna."

Edna tried. She gave us chores to do, taught us table manners, and stepped in when my older sisters, who were twins, had fights. Edna braided my hair every morning and knelt with me when I said prayers at bedtime.

Very early one morning in April, the year I turned seven, Bill came to my room to wake me. "Hurry," he said, "it's the sow's time."

I got into my clothes in the dark, pulling on

my boots with no socks. It was too much trouble finding socks without a light.

The house we lived in was big, with many rooms. It was made of adobe bricks and had red tile floors. I could race down the hall to the main entrance without making a sound.

Bill was waiting for me by the ditch. "I'm ready," I said.

We went down the path through the alfalfa field to the corrals. We passed the barn and kept going toward the pig sheds, a series of low buildings with plank fencing all around.

"She's over here," Bill said, turning right. I knew sows in labor were separated from the rest of the pigs for their own safety and for the well-being of their litters.

Getting into the birthing shed meant crawling on hands and knees through a narrow doorway. I followed Bill and felt my stomach rise at the stench of ammonia and dung.

Bill shone the beam of his flashlight on the sow's face. Her eyes were shut. She breathed in rapid bursts of air that sounded like small explosions going off.

"Look," Bill said. "We're just in time. Here they come."

The piglets emerged from the sow's immense body enclosed in a silvery, slippery skin that looked like a giant soap bubble. Bill used his pocket knife to slit open the skin. The piglets spilled into the straw like pink beads dropping from a broken string.

Bill cut the umbilical cords and squeezed each piglet to be sure it breathed on its own. There were nine in all. Bill made sure no newborn had its nose stuck in the damp and smelly straw.

"Did you bring your bandanna?" he asked.

"No, I forgot."

"Here's mine. Wipe off these babies before they get chilled."

Bill peered into each creased and wrinkled face. The piglets had slits for eyes, and it would be a few days before they were open.

Bill handed me the smallest of the litter. "The runt," he said. "Give that one an extra squeeze."

"Maybe I could help raise this one," I said.

"Runts die, generally."

"If I helped with this one, it might not die," I suggested.

Earlier Bill and I had agreed it was time for me to raise a live animal as part of my 4-H project. I wanted to choose one of the piglets from the spring litters.

"Could be," Bill said. He was preoccupied with another piglet, one with mucus in its nose.

"What do you think, Bill? Could I choose the runt for my project?"

Bill lifted the tiny creature from my hands. He turned it over twice, examining both ends, then he pressed on the runt's chest with his fingers. Apart from its size, the piglet seemed to be fine.

"This one might make it," Bill said. "It might."

"Then, it's okay?"

"Sure."

"Is it a boy or a girl pig?"

Bill took one more look at the runt's back end. "Boy."

"How can you tell?"

"If this isn't a boy pig, then my name isn't Bill Burnham."

When we crawled out of the birthing shed, it was well after sunrise. Magpies and ravens were perched on the rim of the stock tank, calling back and forth to one another.

Before I went to meet the school bus, I asked Bill to keep an eye on my piglet. "I'll be home by four," I told him.

"I think I know that," Bill said, smiling. "Don't you worry. I'll see to things until you get back from school."

I knew this was true. Bill always kept an eye on birthing sows and new litters, as well as colts and calves. It was part of his job.

In school that day it dawned on me that Bill was not my worry. My father was.

My father was away on business a lot. He was away the morning the runt was born. But soon he would return. He would ask questions, wanting to know why I had selected a runt pig for my project. He might object, and if he did, my plans would be ruined.

On the way home I had just one thought: No matter what happens, the runt deserves a name. So I chose one. I called him Jerome.

Project Pig

"You need a plan for your pig if he's going to be a project," Bill told me. It was the afternoon of the same day the sow's litter had arrived. I'd spent the day in school, restless and distracted, wondering how the runt was getting along. I need not have worried. Bill kept an eye on things.

"I don't have a plan yet, but I've named him."

"What's it to be?"

"Jerome William. The second name is in your honor."

Bill grinned at me. His blue eyes were full of pleasure. "I'll be," he said, looking away. "Never did have anything named for me. Where'd the first name come from?"

"I don't know. I just like it. It sounds important."

"Well, now that the name is settled on, it's time to get practical."

Getting practical meant working out a system for seeing to Jerome's special needs. Bill told me it would be best if the runt slept in my room at night. "Be safer that way," Bill said. "Less chance he'll get smothered or starve for lack of a teat."

We set up a wooden crate with straw in the bottom for the bedding.

Bill showed me the proper mixture of milk, water, and liquid vitamin that made up the runt's formula. "The vitamin is the same all young mammals on this ranch get, including you, I'd guess."

I watched closely as Bill screwed a rubber

nipple into a metal cap that fit neatly on the neck of a bottle. The nipple had three holes in it for the milk to flow through.

"What if he doesn't like it?" I asked. "What if he refuses it because he likes his mother's milk best?"

"I never knew a piglet to refuse a meal, but let's try it out. Go get him and bring him here."

We were in the milking room next to the barn. I ran across the yard to the birthing shed and crept in. I was nervous, not sure what the sow might do if one of her babies were removed.

It was no trouble spotting Jerome in the jumble of piglets pressed against the sow's belly. He was the smallest.

I wrapped my hands around his body and pulled gently. There was a popping sound, like a small firecracker going off. It was the runt's mouth coming loose from the sow's teat. The sow kept still. She was asleep.

Back in the milking room I took the bottle from Bill and pointed it at the runt's snout. Nothing happened until I used my fingers to pry apart the animal's jaws. The nipple slid into place, and the sounds of sucking and swallowing filled my ears like music.

"He likes it, Bill. He likes it fine."

A few days later my father was back home. We sat at the supper table, and from my room down the hall came the unmistakable sound of a pig squealing.

"What's that?" my father demanded.

I told him about the arrangement with the runt, and he got angry. My father was a big person. He filled a room. When he got angry, he got bigger. I sat still, feeling afraid, waiting to see what he would do.

"She needs to know this animal," Bill said, breaking the silence. "If she's to show him at the State Fair, she and that pig need to know each other's smell."

"I'll have no pet pigs on this place, and you know it, Bill," my father said, directing his rage away from me for the moment. "No pet pigs."

"We've lost runts when bigger piglets push them off the teat," Bill continued. "This sow has been known to roll on her babies. There's no sense in risking that kind of loss if we can help it."

My father fell silent. Bill had struck a cord. Where there was profit, there was something to consider.

"Project pig?" my father said, staring at me.

"Yes," I said. "Project pig."

"All right. We'll try it. See how it goes."

I took to smuggling Jerome in and out of the house. There was no sense in risking my father's seeing us. It might cause him to change his mind.

Jerome slept well in the crate in my room. I was the one who stayed fitful, listening for snorts or whines that would tell me it was feeding time.

When Jerome was restless and refused to sleep, I sang to him, melodies my mother and Edna had taught me. I hummed into the piglet's ears and soothed him.

Maybe I was making a pet of the runt. I tried not to, but it was impossible not to show my affection.

At six weeks Jerome was big enough to live down at the pig sheds full time. His litter mates were larger than he, but he held his own at one of the sow's teats.

The spring crop of weaners, including Jerome's brothers and sisters, were fated to go to market at twelve weeks of age.

"Jerome won't go to market with the others, right, Bill?" I knew the answer, but wanted reassurance.

"Right," Bill said. "Jerome stays on. He's a project pig."

Two Against One

"Pig farmer! Pig farmer!"

My sisters were twins, two years older than I. They liked to tease. One of them, Tasha, teased me without mercy at the bus stop when news of Jerome spread around the neighborhood.

"She has a new pig," Tasha said, beaming with the pride that comes of being one of the first to know. My other sister, Kim, was the quiet one. She never teased as meanly as Tasha.

"She's got the runt," Tasha said. When she said the word "runt" it sounded like an insult.

My sisters scorned me for the things I loved. It was hopeless to attempt self-defense. Our differences went back as far as we did.

We had never been treated the same by our parents. Baby pictures of the twins showed them in soft dresses, with bows in their fine blond hair. My baby pictures showed a child in overalls and a T-shirt. Early in our lives decisions had been made about how to raise us—and from that time forward I was "the interesting child," in my mother's words, and the twins were "the pretty ones."

My father made rules for me that did not apply to the twins. We all had chores, but mine were to work with Bill down at the corrals or with Edna in the garden. The twins' chores were done inside and supervised by my mother.

I was to wear blue jeans and cowboy boots. My hair was never to be cut, except the bangs, which Edna trimmed on a regular basis. The twins wore dresses and pretty shoes. They went to town to get their hair cut and styled.

My father started me out learning to ride when I was two or three. He said I would learn to be a fine horsewoman. He seemed not to care if the twins rode or not.

One day my father came home from town with a new saddle for me and a Navajo saddle blanket to go with it. It was not my birthday. My sisters hated riding, but they were furious with envy when they saw my new saddle and blanket.

The neighborhood kids were used to my sisters and their teasing ways. I was the one they usually picked on, but there was a girl Tasha hated and tormented; her name was Connie. One of Tasha's favorite tricks was to hold Connie down and stuff grass into her mouth until she choked.

If Bill or Edna caught sight of any torture going on, they stopped it. The twins were scolded and sent to their rooms. "You need time to think about your ugly behavior," Edna used to say.

The twins never did anything wrong in front of my parents. Like me, they were afraid of my father's anger. At times I wondered if my parents had any idea how horrible Tasha could be.

If cross words passed between us in the presence of our parents, my mother came to the defense of the twins. Looking at me, she'd say, "Leave your big sisters alone. Don't be a pest. There are privileges that come with being older."

I considered it unfair and unjust. No wonder I had my own separate friends, kids who never associated with the twins. My own friends understood the way things were, and they did not tease me.

Martha, Junior, and the Gonzales Family

Martha was my best friend. She was my age, but taller than me by an inch. Her long, shiny black hair hung in waves down her back. She had bright eyes and perfect teeth. When the need arose, Martha stood up for me, defended me, even against Tasha. Martha was brave.

The person I stood up for was a small,

shrunken boy named Junior. Junior was our age. He had had polio, a virus that ruined children's lives in those days. The sickness had left him stunted, skinny, and inflicted with a limp. Junior wore a brace and sometimes used a crutch. The brace was paid for by the state.

Junior endured a lot of teasing, especially by a boy named Tony who bragged about how fast he could run.

"Nobody cares about you," I shouted at Tony. "So shut up." In my family it was against the rules to say things like "shut up." Sometimes it made me feel courageous to break a rule.

Junior had been abandoned when he was small. The Gonzales family took him in, though they were very poor. In the mornings at the bus stop, the talk revolved around how odd I was to care about Junior, or how dumb I was to want to raise a pig. The afternoons were different.

We all piled off the bus and went running in fifteen different directions, each person with a mission to accomplish now that school was over for the day. Martha and I went to see the pigs first and to give Jerome his afternoon feed. Then we went to Martha's house.

Martha's mother, Mrs. Salazar, kept tortillas hot on the wood stove for us. After we'd eaten our fill, we walked up the dirt road to Junior's house.

We liked it at Junior's. The house was too small for the number of people living in it, but that didn't seem to matter. The floor was cracked linoleum, with a pattern so faded it was impossible to imagine what it must have once looked like. The mud plaster walls were bare, except for some saints' pictures in wooden frames without glass that Mrs. Gonzales had hung here and there. In spite of how poor she was, with many hungry mouths to feed, Mrs. Gonzales usually had more hot tortillas waiting for us.

Mrs. Gonzales had babies on a regular basis. There was often a new one in the house. Martha and I liked babies. We were frequently hired to look after the little ones. Mrs. Gonzales paid us in brown paper sacks filled with chile peppers, never money.

One afternoon, not long after Jerome's birth, Martha and I knocked on Mrs. Gonzales's screen door.

"Come in, come in," she said warmly. "You've come to see the new baby?" she asked, knowing the answer.

"Yes," we both said at once.

The three of us walked into the back bedroom of the house. "There she is," Mrs. Gonzales said. "There's my baby Rose."

"She's perfect," Martha murmured. I nodded in agreement. We both stared at a tiny, brown-skinned infant tucked into the well-padded bottom of a large cardboard box. The box was set on top of a wide bed.

"Yes," Mrs. Gonzales said. "She's perfect."

In my eyes Mrs. Gonzales was ancient. And yet she was capable of producing one lovely baby after another. When I looked at her, I wondered how she could nurse. How could she make milk? Her arms and legs were bone-thin. There was not a scrap of extra flesh on her body. Her face was sharp, and her eyes sank into shadowy hollows.

I glanced at her chest to see if there was any fullness, the swelling that describes a nursing mother. Mrs. Gonzales was as flat as a pancake.

I started to worry. "Do you need formula?" I asked, thinking that without breast milk Rose might not get enough to eat. Formula was expensive. "I can bring you some. Once I get my allowance, I can go to Sena's Store and buy some. I could even bring milk from home."

Just then Junior came into the room. I heard his approach. His crippled legs made thumping sounds on the wooden floors. "She has plenty of milk for the baby," Junior said. I realized he'd heard my question and was offended by it. Junior was quick to take offense at the things people said, even friends like me.

"I'm sorry," I said. "I just thought . . ."

"She has plenty of milk. Rose has enough to eat," Junior said.

I dropped my eyes. My offer had been rude. "I was just wondering," I said softly.

"We have all we need right now," Mrs. Gonzales said. "Thank you for thinking of us, but we have all we need."

Before leaving, I touched the baby's skin with my fingers. She did not stir.

When we went out into the front yard, I told Martha I was embarrassed by what I'd said. "They're so poor and everything," I said. "I just wanted to help."

"It's true," Martha answered. "They're poor, but they're proud."

The Catholic Church and Me

I wanted to join the Catholic Church, and I had several strong reasons why. One was the way the church smelled—there was a scent of home-made candles and the aroma of wood smoke. The church was heated in winter by a wood stove near the back of the sanctuary. I remembered those smells from the very first times I ever went to church with Martha and her family.

Another reason I yearned to convert and become a Catholic was the way the inside of the church looked. Hanging on the white walls were painted pictures of saints who had soft eyes that gazed down on us where we sat on wooden benches. People were calm and peaceful in church. The oldest ones, grandmothers and grandfathers, murmured prayers while their rosary beads slid smoothly through their fingers.

The main and most important reason I wanted to convert was that being a Catholic would make me be like my friends. Every one of my friends was a Catholic. I was an outsider.

On countless Sunday mornings Martha's family took me with them to church. They and the other people present took communion, confessed, or simply prayed. I sat and watched, wondering what it would be like to be them.

I knew it would be a battle to convince my parents that I wanted to become a Catholic. But when I turned eight, I was ready for the fight.

Edna and Bill were Baptist. I never knew them to go to a church, but it was obvious they had beliefs. Edna was willing to say prayers with me at bedtime. I decided to tell her first about my desire to be a Catholic.

"I want to convert and be a Catholic," I said to her one afternoon. My sisters were out somewhere. I felt safe bringing up the subject.

"What on earth for?" Edna asked. She was surprised at my statement.

"So I can be like my friends," I told her.

Edna turned and looked at me oddly. She rubbed her hands on her apron, a thing she did when she was nervous. Her full, round face turned red. "I see," she said, hesitating. "Well, look. Go and talk to your father. He's the one to talk to about this. Tell him what you've told me. Tell him how you feel about your friends."

A few days later, I found a time.

My father was a well-known architect. His company had offices in New York, Chicago, Dallas, and Portland, Oregon. He was often away, visiting these offices and seeing to his work.

His ranch-office was a small building out in back of the main house. Silver poplar trees helped conceal it from view. My sisters and I, and even my mother, were told never to bother my father when he was absorbed in his work in his office. He did not like being interrupted.

The day I decided to talk to him about my conversion, he was not expecting my knock at the door. My stomach was tight with worry about how he would receive me.

"Who is it?"

"It's me," I said. "Jenny."

"Come in, then," he said. His voice was calm. The sound of it traveled through the wall of fear in my belly.

"What do you want? Why aren't you in school?"

"School's over."

"So, what is it?"

"I wanted to talk—to ask a question."

"Go on, then. Ask it." He pushed back from his desk on a chair with wheels on the feet.

"I want to be converted and become a Catholic."

My father's dark eyes peered out the window at the shadows dancing under the trees. He was quiet for a long moment. When he spoke, his voice was gentle. "If holy water doesn't freeze, I will allow you to become a Catholic. Deal?"

I thought for a second. It seemed reasonable. "Deal," I said. I thought my father was being easy. A person never knew with him. There were times he let me have my own way.

"Holy water is like any other water," Martha said. "It freezes."

I was checking around, asking people who would know. "Holy water freezes," Martha's mother said. "Besides, it isn't right to question these things. It's a sacrilege to doubt the church in any way."

In the end I realized my father was playing a trick. I knew he insisted on raising his children without any religion. "Those beliefs are for the weak-minded," he said. His "deal" about holy water was to show me how foolish I was in my desire. He was making fun of me, and of the Church.

I talked to my mother. "How come I can't be a Catholic?" My mother was more sympathetic than my father. But she had trouble making big decisions. She left heavy matters to him.

"You know your father's wishes when it comes to religion," she answered. "He cannot change. You must learn to accept how he feels."

In the end, I had to accept his decision. I settled on being a visitor to the church on the hill where the pictures of saints watched over the people. I felt I had no choice. At least I could watch the old men and women in black coats and shawls light candles on the altar. I would continue to be with my friends as we stood around the wood stove on a snowy Sunday morning. It was better than nothing.

The Pet Parade

There was an annual event in our town. It was called Fiesta. People celebrated for three days, honoring the conquest of the Spanish over the Indians and of the Anglos over the Spanish.

There were three Fiesta parades. The one I cared about was the pet parade. Every year since I could remember, I'd been in the pet parade. I usually took one of my cats or one of the ranch dogs. Once I took my pony, Polly. She was half-Shetland and quite mean. She almost hurt one of the other children when she kicked up her back feet. After that I never took her again.

The year I had Jerome, I took him. The pet parade came in late summer. I was training Jerome to a leash by then. We were preparing for his appearance at the State Fair. The pet parade would be a dry run for what was to come.

Edna picked out my outfit. The night before the parade she altered one of my older sister's skirts so it would fit me. She ironed a blouse that had ruffles on it. She tied up my hair in rag twists. "Sleep on these, and in the morning you'll have ringlets," Edna promised.

The next morning when Edna undid my rags, my hair fell in thick curls down my back and around my shoulders. Bill fetched Jerome while I dressed in my skirt and blouse. Bill oiled Jerome's hide and tied a red bandanna around the pig's neck. Jerome and I were ready for a parade.

My sisters had never wanted to be in the

parade. They rode into town with my parents in the station wagon. I went in the pickup truck with Bill, Edna, Martha, and Junior. Jerome was in a crate in the back.

The parade started in the Cathedral garden. The children and their animals walked around the plaza, then returned to the garden where the Archbishop himself gave each participant a blessing.

The start went well. Jerome was at my heels, his leash slack. We were more than halfway around the plaza before anything went wrong.

Jerome's attention was captured by the smell of some kittens being wheeled in a doll baby-buggy. A girl about my own age was pushing the buggy. The aroma of cat was too much for Jerome. He made a leap and turned over the buggy, sending the kittens sprawling. The leash slipped from my fingers, and the girl who owned the kittens began to scream bloody murder.

"Jerome William," I cried. "Come back!" It was in vain that I called. I chased him, stumbling over the length of my skirt, hearing it rip. Every time I got near the pig, he changed his direction. A few brave spectators tried to catch him, but his hide was too slick to grasp.

Suddenly I felt the firm grip of a hand on the back of my blouse. I twisted around and looked into the red, hot face of a police officer.

"That your pig?" he asked.

"Yes, sir," I answered, thinking it a stupid question.

Between us we managed to capture the loose Jerome. The officer led us back to his patrol car, which was parked about half a block from the plaza.

"Where are you taking us?" I asked. "To jail?"

"No. To my car. We'll sit this one out. We'll find your folks when it's over."

I was humiliated and angry. The officer refused to let me sit with Jerome. He insisted I sit in the back of his car with all the windows rolled up.

I stared at Jerome, who was forlorn and bewildered on the sidewalk, his leash tied to a parking meter. He was filthy from his rampage in the streets.

"You messed up, Jerome," I muttered. "You messed up big."

The officer waited until all the children and their animals were finished being blessed. He then opened the patrol car door and told me to get out. "Untie that pig and tell me where your family is."

"This your kid?" the officer asked my father.

"She looks familiar," my father said, laughing.

"She's all yours, then," the officer said.

"You're a mess," my mother said, tugging at my blouse. "Look at you. You've torn your skirt."

"She's just fine," my father said. "She did all right with that crazy pig. Tried your best to catch him, didn't you?"

"Yes, I did," I said, looking at my feet. "I did."

On the way back home Bill and Edna both told me I did what I had to do. "Pigs will be pigs," Bill said. Like my father, he was laughing over the whole incident.

"I don't think it was so funny," I said, feeling

hurt. “Everybody thinks it was so funny.”

“I’d have to agree,” Bill said.

“Yes,” Edna said, grinning. “I’d have to say it was a funny sight to see.”

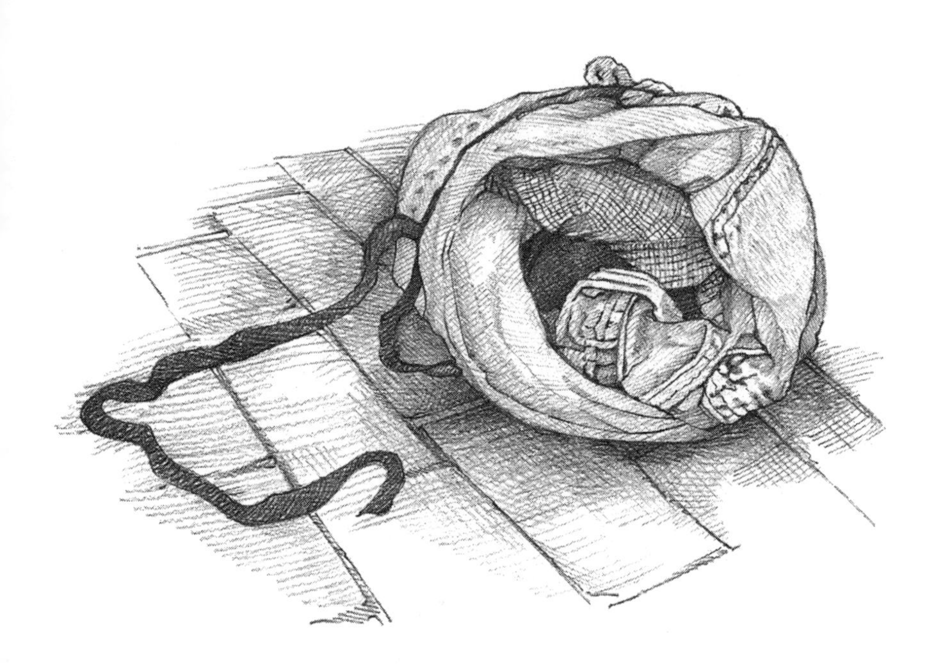

Jerome's Fate Is Decided

My father's objection to "pets" on the ranch, other than the usual cats and dogs, made my relationship with Jerome tricky. I was not a secretive kid, but there were things about the pig I did not want my father to know.

Jerome's fate would be based partly on how well he did as a sire to healthy litters of piglets.

The first time Bill put Jerome in with a willing sow, all Jerome did was sit and stare at her with lazy eyes. He was six and a half months old then.

"I was afraid of something like this," Bill said.

"What do you mean?" I asked, not understanding.

"This animal may be more human than pig," Bill told me. "He's spent so much time with you and your friends, he's not clear on how to be a boar."

"He'll grow into it," I suggested. "He's still too young."

"Let's hope that's it," Bill said.

Bill left Jerome with different sows on several occasions, each time with the same results—no action on the pig's part. I begged Bill to keep trying and not let my father know there was a problem. "If he knows, that's the end of Jerome," I said. Bill promised he would say nothing to anyone about Jerome's inability to perform.

State Fair time was approaching. Jerome might have a chance to win a ribbon because he was well made in his body and beautifully mannered. But he'd never make it that far if my father discovered the truth.

Running away from home had never crossed my mind until I pictured Jerome shot in the head and hanging by his heels from a hook on the barn door. I'd seen other animals this way, and I'd never grown used to it. I'd have to save him from this fate.

I prepared myself at bedtime. I took every piece of clothing I loved and tied them into a tight wad. Then I bound them all together with a length of clothesline. It was the same line that had been Jerome's leash for more than five months. I took soap and my hairbrush from the bathroom. As a criminal slinks away from the scene of a crime, I slipped away from my home, the only one I had ever known.

In darkness that swelled around my head, I crept down the path to the alfalfa field until I came to the barn. A right turn brought me to the pig sheds and the pen where Jerome lived.

"What's up, kiddo?"

It was Bill's voice. What was he doing down here in the dark?

"I came to get Jerome," I said. "We're running away. It's no use trying to stop me. I don't want to go, but I just have to. Otherwise Jerome will be slaughtered."

Bill reached out and put a hand on my shoulder. "No need," he said quietly. "I came down here tonight to check on that pig. He's in with the young sow, Gloria. He did fine. He did his job, finally."

"Oh, Bill, I'm so glad!" I cried. "Then I don't have to run away?"

"I shouldn't think it necessary," Bill said.

We talked then. Bill told me he'd seen what he needed to see, and that a litter would result from Jerome's night with Gloria.

"You can tell my father that Jerome is a normal boar, right, Bill?"

"Looks that way. Jerome will be a breeder. We'll keep him on. He won't get slaughtered. Your father is too wise a man to kill a good piece of pig flesh when it's producing."

We walked up the path together. Bill never appeared to see my bundle tied with clothesline. He never mentioned it again, nor did I.

Becoming a Cowgirl

Everybody around me had a profession. Or else they knew what they would be when they grew up.

Bill was a wrangler and a cowboy. Edna was a cook. Stella Lucero did laundry and cleaned people's houses. My mother was a mother, and my father was an architect and a rancher.

Martha said she wanted to become a nun. Tony wanted to race cars. Ben and Roberto said they would be farmers. Junior wanted to help people like himself. He wanted to be a doctor. My sisters wanted to get married.

Of all the people I knew, I was the only one who had no answer when someone raised the question, "What do you want to be when you grow up?"

I hated cooking. Marriage was not an option I took seriously. My sisters were blond, blue-eyed, and beautiful. Boys liked them—not me.

I had my old mare, Babe. For years we had been pals. I rode Babe with saddles and without. We'd traveled the hills and arroyos together, riding for hours under the sky. I had been in a few horse shows with her. One time we even got second prize in barrel racing.

It dawned on me one day when I was nine: I would be a cowgirl.

As usual, Bill was the first person I told.

"I'm going to grow up and ride beautiful horses in the rodeo and make tons of money."

Bill frowned. He had a bony face that was half-hidden under the brim of his hat. "Money?"

he asked. "This decision you're making is about money?"

"Yes," I said. "Lots of it. And silver buckles, and trophies, and ribbons, too."

"Not a great reason for choosing a profession," he said. "Not strong enough."

We talked about it then, and at other times. I knew Bill wanted me to be good at what I did, whatever it turned out to be. He wanted me to ride well and maybe even be an expert someday. He did not want me to be motivated by money.

"My dad makes money," I said. "That's why he has a ranch."

"Your dad makes money in other ways," Bill told me. "He loses money on this place."

It was the first I'd heard of my father losing anything, especially money. "What about the hay crops? And the corn?"

"Your dad is not doing this ranch for money. He's doing it for love. His architecture is for money."

Bill explained the difference between what a person does for love and what that same person does to make money. When he got through explaining I understood my father a little bit better.

Still, I wanted to be a cowgirl, to ride in the Junior Rodeo and maybe carry the American flag around the arena. I yearned for a shirt with pearl buttons and fringes on the sleeves. I wanted pants that fit tight. I wanted fame and glory in the rodeo arena.

Bill took me to register for the Junior Rodeo.

"Name?" the man asked. He was short, and his shirt had pearl snaps.

"Jennifer Owings."

"Event?"

"Barrel racing."

The man handed me a number painted on a canvas strip. "Pin this to the back of your shirt," he said. "Wear it when you're racing."

During the few days that passed between registration and the rodeo itself, I practiced as if every try would be my last chance to win. Bill helped.

"Tighten up those legs," he called from the side of the corral. "Lean forward more. You lose time sitting back like that."

I loved the wind in my ears, the slapping sound of my legs against Babe's sides, and the certainty I felt that I would outride all the other barrel racers.

The next thing I knew it was time to go to town, to trailer the mare—my beloved Babe. It was time to appear in the ring in front of a crowd of perfect strangers.

I kept close to the entrance gate like the other contestants, circling Babe around and around. I listened for my name over the loudspeaker and almost missed the call when it came because I was so nervous.

"Number thirty-seven. Jennifer Owings, riding her mare, Babe. This young lady will have to ride hard today, folks. We have some mighty fine young barrel racers in this contest."

Maybe if the announcer had not said anything about the stiff competition, or perhaps if I had not made up my mind ahead of time to be a winner, I'd have done better with those barrels. I had trouble keeping my mind on business from the instant Babe shot into the ring at the sound of the starter pistol.

The crowd was screaming, horns were honking, and I slipped up at the second barrel. I hit it with my left boot and over it went, hitting the ground with an empty thud.

"Disqualified!" the announcer said. "Better luck next time, kid."

A girl from Texas won everything. Her horse was a bright and powerful palomino stallion. Her outfit dangled and flashed with fancy fringes and studs. She wore a lime-green cowboy hat, and her smile never left her face, even when she flew around the barrels with reins flying and legs flapping.

I saw her family on the sidelines. They laughed, clapped, and cheered when she rode into the arena to accept the first-place ribbon from the judge's hands.

In spite of being disqualified, I loved the race. A fine, powdery dust stung my nose when I rubbed Babe's sweaty neck and whispered to her that she'd done just fine. "Better luck next time," I told her.

Rose

When winter came, the Gonzales baby, Rose, was three months old. She was round and fat and bright-eyed, with black hair that stuck up on top of her head.

Winter was hard on the poorer people in the valley. Many families heated with wood-fired stoves and lived in their kitchens until spring came. Some families went without enough to eat.

Winter was difficult for Junior. His joints froze up and got more painful than usual. When he got too stiff to make it to school and back, Mrs. Gonzales took him to town for treatments.

The treatments were free, but getting to town was often a problem. Mr. Gonzales worked for the highway department. He was gone a lot, working downstate or up, leaving Mrs. Gonzales without transportation.

One morning in early winter, Mrs. Gonzales came to the bus stop to talk to Martha and me. "Will you look after the little ones for me?" she asked us. "I have to take Junior to town for treatments."

"We'll go after school," I told her.

"I need you there now," Mrs. Gonzales said.

Martha and I looked at each other. Could we miss a day at school? Yes, we wordlessly agreed. We could.

The older Gonzales kids were already climbing on the bus when Martha and I stood and watched Mrs. Gonzales walk away, Junior limping beside her. His crutch hit the ground hard and made a tapping sound. “The baby is alone,” I said. “Let’s go.”

Martha stayed with me all day. We played with the baby and kept the fire going in the wood stove. We didn’t eat anything because there was little to eat. When it got to be four in the afternoon, Martha said she had to go. She left.

At four-thirty Linda came in. She was twelve, with flashing eyes and perfect teeth. “How’s the baby?” she asked me. Then she went out.

Ben, who was ten, came in. Roberto, who was eleven, was close on Ben’s heels. Both boys asked after the baby. I told them she was fine, even though she wasn’t.

From the first hour of looking after Rose, I knew she was not well. Her eyes were lacking their usual brightness. She was extrawarm to the touch. By five, I was up and searching the house for medicine. There was nothing.

When evening came, I lay the whimpering baby down on the big bed, the one where all the older children slept. It was getting cold. I went out back and brought in enough wood to last the night.

Cynthia, the eight-year-old, came home about seven. She helped herself to a cold tortilla and went to bed. I tucked her in because she asked me to.

One by one the others came home. No one talked much. They went to bed without any supper.

Rose had a noise in her chest that worried me. The later it got, the more scared I was. I filled a tin pot with water from a bucket by the back door. I put the pot on the stove and got steam going. It helped, some.

As I held Rose close, I wondered where Mrs. Gonzales was. Could she be frozen by the roadside? Was Junior frozen, too? Why had they not come home? Maybe they'd been murdered or run over by a truck. My father would have had the state police out looking for me by now.

I knew I was in deep trouble, that my father would never understand or forgive me. Still, I had no choice but to stay where I was.

In the night I woke up and rubbed the baby's belly. Edna had done the same for me once or twice. I knew how good it felt.

Morning came with a pale light that lifted me out of my chair and gave me hope. Rose was a rag-doll baby, asleep on my shoulder. I was numb from sitting so long in the same position.

The world outside the window was gleaming with frost. I wondered how the universe could be so frozen and so beautiful at the same time.

I took some cold tortilla and broke it into pieces. I moistened these in the hot water on the stove. I put bits of this nourishment next to Rose's tiny mouth. Toothless as she was, she responded by gnawing on the tortilla and swallowing some. She seemed better.

Just as the older kids were getting up, my father burst into the Gonzales kitchen. He never thought to knock. Mrs. Gonzales, with Junior hobbling behind, followed.

"I caught this woman on the road," my father said. He was pointing at Mrs. Gonzales as if she were a devil from hell. "I've got the police out looking for you," he raged. "You!" he repeated, stabbing a finger in my direction.

Rose began to cry. Cynthia, Linda, Ben, and Roberto hovered in a circle around us and looked frightened.

"I knew Jenny was here," Mrs. Gonzales said calmly. "I knew she would look after things. We couldn't get back sooner because we couldn't get a ride."

Junior nodded his head up and down in exaggerated agreement.

"We spent the night at the hospital. We slept in the waiting lounge," Mrs. Gonzales explained.

There was something entirely otherworldly about her face, the gaunt cheekbones and sunken eyes. She had never considered that there might be a problem with her not letting anyone know of her trouble getting back home. I could see my father was taken aback.

"This makes no sense," he said. "I'm supposed to sit and wonder if my daughter has been kidnapped, or worse, killed, and think nothing of it?"

"I knew she was here," Mrs. Gonzales said. The large brown eyes so deep in her face looked straight into my father's eyes. "I knew she was here."

My father gave up after that. He was stumped. He slammed out the door saying, "You're irresponsible, all of you."

Later, Edna told me I did what I had to do. Bill agreed. "You couldn't take a sick baby out in sub-zero cold," he said.

My father's final remark was to Edna, not me. "See that she doesn't have bedbugs," he told Edna at supper. "Check her tonight."

Edna promised she would.

The Snake Dance

The summer I was nine we took a family trip to the Grand Canyon in Arizona. We drove, and on the way my sister Kim threw up. My father got mad and threatened to turn around and take the bunch of us home. I'd never seen the Grand Canyon, and I did not want to turn around.

"Let's go on, dear," my mother suggested.

"Kim is prone to being carsick, but she'll be fine soon, won't you, Kim?"

I was grateful for my mother's intervention.

We went on, but in the end the Grand Canyon was not my father's true destination. After a single night there, we continued north into the vast wilderness of Hopi country.

It was late August, the time of year the Hopi Indians held their snake dances. My father loved the Indian people. He worshiped them. Watching their dances was as close as he came to a religious experience. He kept a crumpled piece of paper in the glove compartment of the station wagon, a list of where and when certain dances were likely to occur.

Non-Indians could never be sure a dance would happen on the day it was supposed to, nor could they be assured of permission to watch.

Not until I was older did I understand that my father liked this aspect of the Indian culture. He enjoyed it that the Indians were, by nature, enigmatic and mysterious.

At the Grand Canyon we stayed in a motel. But there were no motels in Hopi country. We would sleep on the ground in sleeping bags, a thing I loved. It was something my mother and sisters hated.

After a day of driving, we had arrived and looked for a spot to camp. We found one in the bottom of a wide arroyo about half a mile from the pueblo. Juniper trees grew up the steep sides of the arroyo, all the way to the rim, which stood sharp against a bright, blue sky.

On that first night I lay on my back and watched the stars. Once in a while one of them cut loose and shot across the heavens, leaving a trace of fire behind.

I was too young to understand what we saw on that trip. Even so, I will never forget it. The images are branded in my brain forever.

With a sprinkling of other non-Indian people, my family and I stood on the sidelines to watch the dance.

Hopi men, their bodies painted black with white streaks, filed down a narrow dirt street into the dance area. They wore moccasins with fringes on the ankles. Their groins were covered by red woven fabric, decorated with black and white designs. Some carried straps of leather with white shells tied in rows, shells that clapped with every dance step.

Most of the dancers carried live snakes. Some had snakes in their mouths, while others wore snakes as bracelets around their arms or as necklaces on their necks. For every dancer with a snake, there was another who moved behind with one hand on the snake man's shoulder. The men who followed held sticks with feathers attached. They waved these sticks in front of each snake's face.

I knew many of the snakes were rattlers. I'd heard that noise before. A childhood in northern New Mexico meant being familiar with venomous creatures, including rattlesnakes.

When a dancer pressed the face of a fanged rattlesnake close to his cheek, I cried out. It was a low cry, and no one took any notice.

The women had built an altar out of cottonwood branches. At the base of the altar a hole had been dug in the earth, a pit where the snakes were kept. The pit was the source, the place the dancers went to lift out the snakes they danced with.

The second day of watching was the same as the first, except something went wrong.

My father was restless from the moment he woke up and ate a breakfast of cold cereal with canned milk. In the pueblo, standing five in a row as we had the day before, I again sensed my father's troubled mind. Suddenly he took off, walking slowly at first, and then faster, in the direction of the altar and the snake pit.

He elbowed his way through the slender line of spectators. He didn't get far. A heavy-shouldered Indian moved in quickly and took my father by the upper arm. A second Indian appeared and took my father's other arm. Between the two Indians my father looked odd, like a puppet that had lost its strings.

The Indians led my father off. They gestured to my mother and the rest of us to follow—which we did.

Three more Indians came and surrounded us. Nobody said a word, but it was clear what was expected. We were to pack up and be on our way. We were no longer welcome.

On the way home my father was silent and

broody. I felt sorry for him. I knew he yearned to be a part of the magic of the dance. Maybe he felt the way I did about wanting to be a Catholic. It was something he could not achieve.

The Drowning

During the autumn I was nine, there were two funerals in the valley. One was for an old person and the other for someone very young.

Martha's great-grandfather, old Lolo, passed away. At the wake given by Mr. and Mrs. Salazar, he looked more asleep than dead. He was flat on the sofa in the front room of the house, dressed in his best shiny blue suit. I shivered when I looked at him. It was a shock to see someone dead.

Women nearly as ancient as Lolo circled the sofa, their black clothes rustling. They said prayers and fingered their rosary beads. I heard one say Lolo was past one hundred when he breathed his final breath.

Old Lolo was buried under a ponderosa pine way up in the mountains. The family could not afford a town burial.

The sadness and surprise I felt when Lolo died was nothing compared to what I felt when death came for Baby Rose.

Rose was barely one year old when she toddled off and fell into the irrigation ditch. Mrs. Gonzales was hanging wash at the time. She could not have known the ditch was running full. Even if she had known, she never caught sight of her baby daughter heading for disaster.

"It took minutes," Linda said.

"It took seconds," Ben insisted.

"No time at all," Roberto agreed.

I listened to what they said and cried inside, my heart completely broken.

Rose had been so fond of Jerome. She loved

it when I held her up so she could ride on the pig's hairy back. Martha and I had taken turns toting Rose around the neighborhood before she was able to walk. We held her hands when she took her first steps on her own. We spent our allowance on dresses for Rose, fluffy ones we found at the dime store for a dollar and a half apiece, two dollars at the most.

Rose laughed easily. She liked crawling across our lawn chasing grasshoppers. Before she knew these insects tasted terrible, she tried to eat them.

My mother loved it when I brought Rose over for a visit. I'd take the baby to the kitchen, where Edna would brush the thick, dark hair away from Rose's grubby little face. "Pretty babies ought to have clean faces," Edna used to say, wiping Rose's nose and mouth with a damp cloth.

Then Rose was gone, her memory left behind like an afterglow, the kind that hangs in a dusty sky when summer lightning flashes.

The whole neighborhood came to the wake. It was held in the Gonzales kitchen. The old wooden table was weighted down with donated food. The wood stove was fired, even though it wasn't cold yet.

I watched Mrs. Gonzales at the wake. I stared at her face. I saw that she blamed herself, not God, for the death of her baby daughter.

Edna was there, and Bill, too. My mother came and paid her respects, holding and gently shaking Mrs. Gonzales's thin hand.

Rose was laid out on the big bed in the back bedroom. Junior stood guard at the door, watching each person come and go. He turned his face away when I went in and kissed Rose on the cheek. She was dressed in white, with white socks and white baby shoes. I squeezed her finger and told her good-bye.

I went with the Gonzales family to the mountains for the burial. They invited me and Martha. We rode together in the back of a cousin's pickup truck. The night air blew straight into the ache in my soul. Thinking of Rose cradled in her mother's arms, riding in another pickup ahead of us, brought the tears back to my eyes.

The men dug a hole in the ground by the

light of the truck headlamps. There was no moon, only the rustlings of invisible creatures in the forest all around. Mrs. Gonzales, with her husband close, placed the child's body in a wooden box Mr. Gonzales had made. A few words were muttered in Spanish. All the mourners, including me, crossed themselves. The box was lowered into the earth, dirt was thrown in, and Rose was gone.

Mr. Gonzales, who did woodworking on the side, had fashioned a tiny cross for his youngest child. On the crosspieces he had burned her name: Rose Antonia Maria Gonzales.

Stella Lucero, the Witch

Stella Lucero had red hair and green eyes. No one knew her exact age. She did laundry for many of the families in the valley, including mine.

Stella claimed the ability to shift her shape and become an owl. She said she was a witch. “The good kind, generally,” she added.

I admired Stella. She knew a lot about life,

and she was wise. I could tell this from the way her eyes flashed when she talked.

There were times I was puzzled by what she told me. Once she said to beware of Jerome. "Watch out for that pig," she told me. "He may not be what he seems."

"What do you mean?" I asked.

Stella shook her head and looked at me strangely. "Sadness is there. I sense it. I cannot say more."

Sometimes Martha and I went to the trees by the dam where Stella said she perched or flew around when she was being an owl. In vain we searched the leafy branches of the cottonwoods, trying to spot an owl with green eyes.

After Rose Gonzales died, it was Stella who comforted me. "It's not fair," I said. "To make a life and then end it."

"Lo que no se puede remediar, hay que aguantar," Stella answered. "What cannot be remedied must be endured."

Stella was not married. She had no children, but she had many relatives in the valley. She had cousins and nephews. One afternoon a young cousin named Miguel came to her door. "I need your help," he said.

Miguel explained that he was going to become a member of the Penitente Brotherhood. Martha and I were visiting Stella when Miguel came by. We were sitting at the kitchen table in her house, and we listened to what they said.

"Do you know what you are doing?" Stella asked the boy. "Are you aware of the consequences?"

"Yes," Miguel said. "My brothers and my father are members of the Brotherhood. I am seventeen now. It is time for me to join."

Stella nodded. "So, you've thought about this."

"Yes," Miguel told her. "It would shame me if I didn't join."

The Penitente Brotherhood Miguel wanted to join was a Catholic society for men. The members were secretive. They kept their rites hidden from view behind the thick adobe walls of their meeting place, a building called the Morada.

The Brotherhood did good deeds for people. When a family needed money for food, a Brother could be called upon to help. If someone got sick, a Brother might pray for them or light a special candle at the altar in the Morada. The Brothers held rosary services at wakes for the dead and raised money to pay for the baptism of new babies.

Anglos were not supposed to know anything about the Penitente Brotherhood, particularly what went on inside the Morada. What Anglos knew came to them through a system of gossip and rumors. I knew the Brotherhood believed in rites that caused some of the members to bleed from self-inflicted wounds. I had heard that Brothers hurt themselves at Easter time to honor the suffering of Jesus.

Everything about the Brotherhood was shrouded in a veil of secrecy and question, unless you were one of them.

Stella, like the rest of us, suspected that the initiation rite was bloody and brutal. She wanted to make sure her young cousin knew what he was getting into. "Why do you come to me?" she asked him. "What do you need me for?"

"I need you for the aftermath," Miguel answered. "For the part after."

I caught Martha's eye, and she mine. So, it was true. The initiation into the Brotherhood was hard.

"Go on," Stella said. "Tell me more."

"I would like to use your salve, the ointment you call *Enserada.* Others have used it. It heals wounds."

"Yes?" Stella looked at Miguel with a stare that described a stubborn person, someone willing to offer her services only if she knew more about why they were needed.

"Tia," Miguel said. "Tia, you want details I am not allowed to give you. The initiation of a Brother is a secret rite. Believe me, *juntate a los buenos y seras uno de ellos.*"

"What did he say?" I asked Stella. "What does that mean?" I asked Miguel.

"It means, when you get together with good people, you will become one of them," Stella answered.

Stella turned back to Miguel and said, "So, you will have cuts?"

"Yes."

The night of Miguel's initiation came. It was

Good Friday. The moon shone bright and clear in the sky, its gentle light reflecting off the mud walls of the windowless Morada.

Miguel went into the Morada alone. Martha and I hid behind a wooden fence some distance away. We watched the small Morada door to see what might happen next.

Much later, after I had fallen into a sleepy daze, Martha shook me and said, "Look! Here he comes."

Miguel emerged from the building. He wore no shirt, and we could see his back was bleeding. We went to him and offered to help, but he pushed us away.

For three days no one saw him. Not even his own parents knew where he was. It was a part of the initiation to heal oneself and accept help from no one.

On the fourth day Miguel turned up at Stella's. Martha and I knew this because we'd kept a watch going.

At her door Stella told us, "Beat it. He isn't ready for visitors yet. He's sleeping."

Each day after school we went by Stella's to

see how things were. After three days passed, she let us in. "Come on," she said. "He's feeling much better."

There were twelve cuts in the smooth boy-flesh of Miguel's back. One for each Station of the Cross. The salve Stella smeared on him worked wonders. He would have scars, but they would not be too deep.

"Now I believe you are a witch," I told Stella.

We were sitting around the bed where Miguel was recovering. A warm spring breeze made the lace curtain at the window rise and fall.

"Me, too," Martha said. "You have healed Miguel."

"Well, let me tell you this, little girls. When Miguel is back on his feet, I am going on vacation. I will be an owl on my vacation."

We laughed then. All of us, even Miguel, who had not laughed for many days. We laughed until our bellies hurt.

Miguel refused to answer my questions about his initiation. "None of your business," he told me. I knew he was right, but I still yearned to know all the details.

A few weeks later Martha and I were exploring up by the dam. We caught a quick glimpse of an owl resting on a cottonwood branch with its eyes tightly closed.

The Fool

The first real bicycle I had, a two-wheeler, was red and white, a single-speed Schwinn with mud flaps. The fringes on the handgrips waved in the wind.

My grandfather had given me the bike the year I turned eight. He lived with us that year. My grandmother had died, and he was lonely for family.

My grandfather helped me learn how to ride my new bike. He took me up the dirt road to a stretch that ran almost a mile without a bend. We put a leash on Jerome and brought him along. I tied the pig to a fence post so he could sit in the shade and watch.

My grandfather loped alongside while I learned to balance myself and brake without falling. When I could do these things alone, he stood next to Jerome and cheered me on.

My first three solo rides went well. On the fourth one I crashed into the trees by the fence line. I got scratched up, but the bike was fine.

My grandfather had his own bike. It was a lot like mine, only bigger. We took rides up the road to Sena's Store. If it wasn't too hot, we took Jerome with us, his leash tied to my handlebars. I used to spend my allowance at Sena's, getting candy that was bad for my teeth.

In our valley there was a boy people called a fool. They were nice to him; they knew he was not like the rest of us. Once when my grandfather and I rode up to Sena's Store, the fool was there, hanging out around the gas pumps.

The fool was holding on to the handlebars of an ancient bike. It had no back tire guard, and the front one was bashed in.

Inside the store I asked Mr. Sena who had given the fool the bike. Mr. Sena was one of a handful of grown-ups who saw to it that the fool had enough to eat and a place to sleep on cold winter nights.

"Church folks got together," Mr. Sena told me. "Eddy Romero found that old bike in a junkyard in town. Now the fool thinks he can ride to the ends of the earth. He rides that thing up and down, up and down, all day long. He never quits, unless it's to come in here and beg for candy."

"He must love that bike," I said.

I watched the fool from the store window while Mr. Sena and my grandfather talked. The fool was staring in my direction, as if hoping I'd come out and ride with him. I might have, but I was afraid of him.

As far as anyone knew, the fool did no harm. At times he exposed himself. He undid his ragged pants to show us how far he could pee.

That was the worst he ever did. Even so, we were all afraid of him.

When we left Sena's that afternoon, my grandfather waved to the fool and got no response. The fool turned his face away, his brow heavy with a frown, and rode off on his rusty bike.

Some time after that, I learned the fool's bike had been stolen. He had gone down by the river to wade, leaving it propped against a tree. When he came back, the bike was gone.

"It was stupid of him to leave a bike that way," my father said at supper.

"It was a dumb bike," I said. "It wasn't worth stealing."

"The boy isn't all that bright," my mother said, rolling her eyes.

"Nevertheless, he ought not to have left it that way," my father said.

One week later I made a decision.

I rode to Mr. Sena's store alone. My note was written in a clear hand. It said, "I am giving my bike to the fool. He needs it more than me. Signed, a neighbor and a friend."

I tied the note to the handlebars with kite

string and wheeled the bike to Mr. Sena's back door. It was the door he used to come and go, every day of his life. My plan was for Mr. Sena to find the bike first. He could read, and the fool could not. If Mr. Sena discovered the bike before anyone else, my plan would work.

It did.

"So," Mr. Sena said a few days later. "You've given your bike to the fool? You walk to my store now?"

"Yes," I said, feeling hot and tired. "I walk."

"That is good," Mr. Sena said. "That is very good."

I looked at Mr. Sena's face, at his thick eyebrows that met over his nose, and his several chins. I wondered what he meant by how good it was that I walked.

"How come it's good that I walk?" I asked him. "What's good about it?"

"The fool is happy, do you agree?"

"Yes, I think so," I said.

"You are strong and able to walk, yes?"

"That's true," I said.

"All is well," Mr. Sena said.

I never told Mr. Sena what it felt like to be without my bike. Telling him this would not fit into his notion of how good everything was.

My parents, especially my father, questioned my giving the bike to the fool.

"You've gone too far this time," my father told me.

"Maybe," I said. We were at supper. My mother didn't say anything, but my grandfather did.

"It was her bike to do with as she pleased," my grandfather said.

"True enough," my father replied. "She'd better not expect another bike. That's all I can say."

Flash Flood

My friends and I knew places across the river, in the hills, where tarantulas lived in burrows. Sometimes we found snake dens under sage bushes. One summer we found nothing much because it rained every afternoon. It rained so much the animals went off to find higher ground—to keep from being flooded out of their underground homes.

A good thing about the rains was that I saw grasses growing out of the prairie, grasses I'd never seen before in my life. I wondered where the seeds came from. I asked Bill about it. "Those seeds have been in the ground all along," he told me. "The rains make them sprout."

That summer the August rains came in July and lasted until September. Thunderstorms blew over the mountains in the east, bringing rains that saturated the ground and made the ditches overflow. Arroyos ran with cream-colored water. Soggy clumps of gray-green tumbleweed had to be pulled out so they wouldn't clog the culverts.

During times of heavy rains, Martha and I walked up to the highway bridge to wait. What we waited for was the start of the flash flood. That wet summer there was a flash flood nearly every day, always in the evening near dusk.

Adults came to the bridge, too. There was always an audience on the bridge at flood time. It was a trick to know when the water would appear. The heaviest flow came from the high mountains, so there was no telling how long it would take to reach the valley.

When it came, it brought with it any number of drowned pigs, old car parts, and once a ponderosa pine that tossed on the surface like a stick.

That summer the rain gods kept the best for last. People said, "There won't be another flash flood like the one we saw last week." But the rain gods knew better.

There was a day in late August when some of us were standing on the bridge, waiting. We faced east, the direction the flood came from. The water rounded the bend just above where we stood. We turned and raced to the opposite side of the bridge to watch the water head toward the Rio Grande, five miles west.

Suddenly there came a cry. . . . A cry?

At first it seemed impossible, and for several moments I dismissed it as imaginary. Then it came again. The cry was coming from underneath the bridge.

Martha ran with me to the end of the bridge. There we could peer below and see the underparts. To our astonishment we saw the fool, the idiot. He was clinging to the wire that wrapped a piling. He was screaming for his life as swirls of brown water crept up his pant legs and neared his waist.

Surely it was the most water we'd seen all season—the flood the fool managed to get himself caught in.

Cars and pickup trucks were parked on the roadside so passengers could enjoy watching the flood. Out of this seemingly random assortment of spectators and vehicles, my father appeared.

He had a rope around his middle and over his shoulder. He carried the extra length in his right hand. When he plunged his heavy body into the stream, he swayed dangerously against the power of the flow. People watched, spellbound, as my father's efforts brought him, ever so slowly, to the side of the terrified fool.

My father circled the boy with rope. He pried the child's fingers off the wire and tugged hard. The fool fell away from the piling and vanished under the surface of the water.

The boy quickly resurfaced, still screaming.

He thrashed and flailed the air with his arms all the way to the bank.

A crowd formed around the drenched, half-drowned fool. He gasped and spat out brown water, but he appeared to be fine.

My father undid the rope and freed himself from his connection to the fool. As he did so, he scolded the child. "A fine place to play, under a bridge in flood season!"

No one paid any attention to what my father said. Some of the men came up and shook his hand. Mr. Sena approached and said, "Thank you for your courage. God bless you."

I went to my father and hugged him. I wanted him to know I was proud. Of all the people standing around watching, it was my own father who got a rope out of his truck and saved the boy.

My parents set up an educational fund for the fool. We found out he had once been baptized. It was Mr. Sena who gave us the details. The boy's name was Enrique Jesus Rene Sanchez.

"He's related to me, somehow," Mr. Sena said. "That is why I give him a place to sleep in the back of the store on cold nights. That is why I look after him, some."

I was bewildered by my father's willingness to help the boy, a child he had previously referred to as "someone who ought never to have been born" and "a brat." One evening at supper I dared to ask.

"How come you're helping him out?"

"I'd sooner not," my father said, avoiding my eyes. "But when you save a life, you have a responsibility. That's all there is to it."

After this incident we never again called the boy a fool. We used his name, Enrique.

Ballet Lessons

My father liked to say that "suffering is character building." If I told him suffering was cruel and pointless, he said, "Not if you learn a lesson from it. People get tough if they suffer enough."

We seldom agreed because he always insisted he was right.

When I was ten, a certain form of suffering began in my life. I was forced to take ballet lessons. The instructor lived in our part of the valley. He was a friend of my parents. He told them it would be good for me to take ballet. "It will make her more graceful," he said.

Even Edna agreed. "Every little girl wants to take ballet," she said. "It won't do you any harm."

The instructor's name was Jacques. He was from Paris, France. When he first came to the valley, he was considered exotic and strange. He used to talk about his homeland. No matter how much he described it, the place never seemed real to me.

In those days we kids were expected to get places on our own. We were rarely driven unless it was a special occasion or an emergency.

Once my sister Tasha broke her arm in a fall from a horse. That time we all drove into town together, and Tasha got a cast on her arm.

Usually it was not that way at all. "You'll get yourself to your lessons," my father announced. "Or else you'll hear from me about it."

Even though he was away a lot, my father had a gift for knowing what we were up to. He did not miss much. Sometimes I wondered if he had spies watching us, people we knew nothing about and never saw.

I rode Babe to my ballet lessons. Martha came along, riding double behind me. Jerome usually came, too. Jerome was so accustomed to traveling around with me that he was more of a ranch dog than a ranch pig.

Martha waited for me under a cottonwood tree in Jacques's front yard, keeping an eye on the horse and the pig.

Jacques had converted the front room of his house into a dance studio. Mirrors were hung on the walls. I could watch myself stumble and do badly. Early on in my lessons, the other kids stopped bothering to laugh at me. Maybe they took pity on me.

I was the worst in the class from the start, and this humiliated me. Jacques, who insisted we use his first name, was impatient with my pleading. "Don't make me do this," I begged.

"Do not complain this way," he said. "You will do better. You are bound to do better. Be patient."

I asked my parents to allow me to quit ballet lessons. "I'm not good at it," I said.

"I'll be the judge of that," my father replied. Then he asked me how I'd feel about piano lessons.

"Piano?" I was stunned. "Me, take piano?"

"You heard me," he said. "Take your pick, piano or ballet."

I chose ballet. If I had to experience lessons in something, I wanted these to be physical, where I could use my arms and my legs.

Six months went by, with all of my Saturday mornings lost to ballet lessons. In this time Jacques smiled at me twice, once when I showed I knew some positions, another time when I bowed nicely at a recital for parents.

Spring came. What had been difficult in winter became nearly impossible in springtime. I desperately wanted to be playing outdoors, not confined to a room with mirrors at both ends.

It came time for Jacques to select dancers for special events coming up in the summer. Dancers were needed for the bandstand in the plaza and as entertainment during the time between events at the rodeo.

Jacques made his selections, saving me for

last. "You will be a Gloomlet during Fiesta," he told me.

I heaved a sigh of relief. Maybe this was something I could do well. At the very least I would practice hard. I vowed to try to be the best Gloomlet ever.

In our town, Fiesta was launched with the burning of a giant puppet called Zozobra. The name means "old man gloom." The burning of Zozobra signaled the end of gloom for another year.

Members of the Elks Club and troops of Boy Scouts built the forty-foot high puppet out of endless rolls of crepe paper. Zozobra was wired into a standing position in one of the town parks. His mouth was made to open and close. His arms could be lifted and dropped, and his eyeballs rolled around in their sockets.

Hundreds of people came to see Zozobra burn. Families came with picnic suppers. People spread tablecloths on the grass and waited for dusk, when the fire would begin.

There were twenty Gloomlets, ten on Zozobra's right and ten on his left. Each

Gloomlet was dressed as a ghost, and each was expected to act the part, weaving this way and that in a ghostly manner. A recording of moans and groans was played on a loudspeaker to lend credibility to the entire scene.

Jacques was the fire master, a role I know he enjoyed because of the way he leapt and twisted in the air. It was the fire master who lit the puppet and started the blaze. Jacques wore red tights, a red shirt, and a red hood with feathers on top. He carried a torch in each hand. His wild and frenzied dance ended only when the flames reached Zozobra's chin.

Edna helped me with my costume. She cut eyeholes in a bedsheet. It was important that no one know the exact identity of a Gloomlet. The sheet was my disguise.

"I can't dance right," I told Edna. I was practicing on the front lawn, and she was helping me. "I don't know how to keep from tripping."

"Do this," she said, standing and showing me. "Turn like this, see?"

I laughed because Edna, who was round and

fat, looked funny dancing like a ghost in her housedress and apron.

With Edna's help and her patience, I began to get the knack of what to do without falling down.

Near the end of one of our practice sessions, Bill came up from the corrals. He was smelly from loading manure. "Here's my advice, kid. Don't go and get yourself burned up along with Zozobra."

The night came, a Friday. I stood waiting with the other Gloomlets, all dressed exactly like me. It crossed my mind that these were children like me, kids who did poorly in ballet, but who achieved their shining moments as Gloomlets.

We were arranged according to our height, with the little ones on the ends. The audience of folks on the grass cheered as we filed into position. Jacques flew into view from the sidelines, waving his fires and landing with a thump on the platform in front of the puppet.

Jacques danced as if it were his last chance to do so. People called out, Zozobra's recording of moans filled the air, and my humiliation of months passed began to fade away.

It was splendid. It was glorious. I loved it that no one other than my family and friends knew who I was. To the people watching, I was a Gloomlet, and that was enough.

I was sad when Zozobra burned. I had come to like his red-lined mouth and the way his eyeballs revolved. I felt sorry for him.

When Jacques lit the fire, tears came to my eyes. The heat of the flames hit me like a blast furnace, and I remembered Bill's warning. Despite the heat and sparks that flew in the air like crazed fireflies, I held my ground.

"You looked weird," Tasha told me at breakfast the next morning.

"She was supposed to look weird. That's what Gloomlets do," my mother said.

Moved by my triumph of the night before, I decided to ask one more time to be allowed to quit ballet. "I liked being a Gloomlet," I said, looking at my father. "But I still hate ballet."

He didn't say anything right away. I held my breath. Maybe there was hope after all.

"What do you think, Emmy?" he asked my

mother. "Do you think this experiment has gone far enough?"

"Yes, dear, as a matter of fact, I do. I think we ought to let her stop the lessons if she so badly wants to."

That was the last anybody said about ballet or any other kind of lessons.

Alternative School

My sister Kim, one of the twins, was in my grade at school. I was nine and she was eleven the year we shared the same teacher. Kim stuttered and had trouble with reading and numbers. The teachers told my parents she ought to be kept back, and so she was.

I liked it that she was in the same room with

me. Kim never teased me unless Tasha was close by. Kim needed to be urged, or she left me alone. She was not a mean person.

If the kids made fun of her, I tried to stop them. Mrs. Simms, our teacher, put my desk next to Kim's so I could help her with the work.

One day Mrs. Simms made all the children read before the class. We did not have to memorize, we just had to read in a clear, strong voice a selection of our own choosing. Kim's turn came, and she couldn't do it.

"Please, Kim," Mrs. Simms said. "We are all waiting." Mrs. Simms spoke in a firm, angry voice, just the kind that would make Kim's fears worse. "I do not want to have to fail you on this exercise," Mrs. Simms added. "Read to us, Kim."

Silence filled the room to bursting. Kim stood next to her desk as we were all expected to do. She said nothing. The look in her eyes was that of an animal startled by a gunshot.

"I will give you one more minute," Mrs. Simms said. "Then you will sit down and accept a failing grade for this exercise."

The classroom full of children heaved a

collective sigh of shame. Mrs. Simms was going too far. All of us knew Kim was a special child, someone different from the rest of us. We knew it was wrong to treat her as Mrs. Simms was doing.

I glared at Mrs. Simms with eyes that would have dropped her in her tracks if eyes could do this. She was looking at her wristwatch, counting seconds.

"I'll read for Kim," I said, jumping up. "I'll read for her." I pushed Kim into her seat and took the book she was supposed to read from. I began, " 'Once there was a moo-cow, moo-cow moo-cow. Once there was a moo-cow I knew very well.' "

"Sit down, Jenny. Sit this instant." Mrs. Simms was furious.

"I'm going to read for her," I repeated.

"You will do no such thing. If you do not sit this minute, it will mean a failing grade for you as well."

"Kim can't read out loud, and you know it." I shot the words across the room without thinking of the consequences. It took no time at all for Mrs. Simms to charge up the aisle between two rows of desks and grab me by the extra material at the nape of my neck.

"Run!" I screamed. Kim ran.

On the way down the hall to the office, Mrs. Simms kept saying I would be expelled. "Expelled!" she shouted in my ear. I did not care. I knew what the word meant. Other kids had been expelled for worse crimes. She could expel me all she wanted. I hated her for what she'd done to Kim.

That night at supper there was a family discussion. "So, you've been expelled from school?" my father said.

"Yes," I answered. I was almost proud of this fact.

"And your sister Kim is on probation?"

"Yes."

A few more questions were asked, and when supper was over my parents went into their bedroom to talk. The rest of us—Bill, Edna, my sisters, and me—waited in the kitchen.

We kept still and quiet, even Tasha, who usually had something to say about everything. Bill and Edna were as somber as I'd ever seen them.

A decision was made. We would be pulled from public school. "This system is not working for my children," my father said.

"You will work at home for now," my mother said. "Edna, you can help."

"Of course," Edna said.

"We'll find a solution soon," my mother added.

The solution was an alternative school twenty miles north of the ranch. It was pretty country, with bluffs the color of cream and piñon-pine-covered hills. A nearby hot springs gave the school its name, the Ojo Caliente School.

One of the teachers lived near enough to drive us both ways each day, a thing my father liked. He did not even mind that the owners and operators of the school were Mormon. "They can be cannibals for all I care," he said. "As long as they educate these children."

Since that terrible day in school, Kim had not spoken. My parents did not show worry. In our new school Kim continued to be completely silent. Her fear-filled eyes were alive with observation of the changes we were going through, but she spoke not a single word.

There were nineteen kids enrolled at the Ojo school. The students ranged in age from five to sixteen. We did everything together, as if we were a single organism, not nineteen separate ones.

I have vivid memories of the Ojo school, mostly because I was one of the youngest kids, and that meant getting tortured.

A much bigger boy, one of the teenagers, grabbed me and hung me by the ankles on a regular basis. He shook me until the contents of my pockets fell to the ground. He then dropped me, took my belongings, and ran. There was no Martha to defend me.

I began going to school with only the clothes on my back. I got so nervous that I started hiding personal treasures around the house, on the unlikely chance this horrible boy would come to visit.

We were taught unusual things, such as how to be reincarnated as a rose bush or a mouse. These were not necessarily Mormon teachings.

They were more the personal beliefs of the people hired to lead our classes.

A Pueblo Indian woman named Maria Martinez came to show us how to make pots. She was a famous potter. Because she lived down the road from us, I'd known her all my life. I loved it that she taught us her art. Hers was my favorite class.

One of the teachers used to take us on field trips into the canyons along the Rio Grande river. We went in search of rock art, those pictures on stone made by ancient people. As we explored among the rocks, the teacher told us stories about how the ancients had lived their lives. This was my second-favorite class.

Our math teacher, who also taught something she called "philosophics," was an elderly widow named Mrs. Murphy. She did her best to teach me the times tables. I learned seven times three, and six times six. She made me memorize long, boring poems with words I did not understand. One day she insisted I memorize the Twenty-third Psalm. This I did well, and I even enjoyed it.

All the teachers and Mr. and Mrs. Gordon, the owners, urged Kim to speak again. She refused. Tasha and I became her voice. We interpreted for Kim and spoke on her behalf when there was a need. It was plain to Tasha and me that Kim intended never to speak again as long as she lived.

We stayed at the Ojo school for a year. Then my parents re-enrolled Tasha and me in public school in town. They kept Kim home and hired a tutor, hoping this would give Kim the time she needed to consider talking out loud.

Another year passed without Kim's speaking. Martha, Junior, and I used to go home after school and tell Kim stories about what happened on the bus or in the classrooms and playground.

"The fat bully touched me on the leg," Martha said once.

"Ugh! What did you do?" Junior asked, making a terrible face.

"I screamed, of course," Martha answered. She laughed. "I screamed, and one of the teachers came and scolded the fat boy. The teacher rescued me."

Kim loved these stories. She listened and kept silent.

Finally, she did speak again. The old stutter was still there, but everyone accepted it. We knew Kim would talk with a stutter all her life. Even my father, who hated imperfections in his children, never gave Kim a hard time about the way she talked.

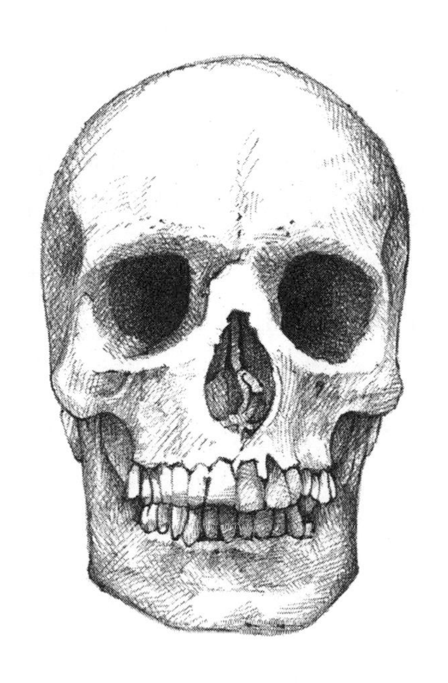

Esteban and First Love

His name was Esteban Gabaldon. He was twelve, and I was eleven. His family moved into the valley from up north. Rumor had it that his father went broke. The family had come from the valley in the first place, so their return was like coming home.

Esteban had a mother, a father, two older brothers, and a younger sister. One morning the kids turned up at the bus stop. The instant I saw Esteban, I knew he would be lucky for me and be my friend.

I loved Junior, but I was not in love with him. I loved other people, even Tasha. But when I met Esteban, I experienced a new dimension of feeling I had never known before.

He and I started to do things together after school. Martha and Junior usually came along. Martha had no special feelings about Esteban, but she never teased me about mine.

The Gabaldon family kept some goats, chickens, cows, and a few hogs. Esteban knew about animals. He liked helping me when I brushed Jerome's hide or took the pig for walks on his leash.

We dug tunnels in the hills. We went to the river and built cities of mud. We tracked coyote and spent hours in the hay barn.

The barn was good on cold, wet days or on snowy days when the sky seemed to be hanging on our shoulders. We carved a fort out of the sweet-smelling hay bales. Bill said we could, as long as we didn't bring all the bales down on top of our heads. We crawled into our fort and curled into wads, with our boot-toes close to our noses.

I allowed Esteban to ride my mare, Babe. When my father found out, he was furious, and I got a scolding. "You know the rules," he said angrily.

It was impossible to explain the rules to Esteban without hurting his feelings. Hispanic children were not supposed to swim in our pool or ride on our horses. Martha could ride double with me, as long as she was in the back and I was in the front.

Esteban acted as if it was not a big deal. "I could care less," he said. "It doesn't bother me."

I believed him.

I never wanted Esteban to touch me. It was not that kind of love. I admired him for his strength, and I figured he was brave. He was good-looking, with a well-made body and the kind of eyes I liked, eyes that were dark and shiny. His hair was thick and black, like Indian hair. He had perfect teeth, and he smiled a lot.

On one especially hot day the three of us—

Esteban, Martha, and me—walked down to the bend in the river where flash floods had carved out a cave. It was a tight curve, and the water was powerful enough to change the shape of the bank again and again.

We found some shade under the steep bank at the center of the bend. The sand was fine under our feet. We took off our shoes and wiggled our toes in the soft grains. We made animal tracks. Martha was an elk, I was a jackrabbit, and Esteban was an antelope.

Something caught my eye, a thing stuck in the bank. It looked like a doorknob. "What's that?" I asked, pointing.

"Don't know," Martha said, going on with her track making.

I went closer, and Esteban followed. He rubbed the thing with his fingertips and made it shine. Together we began to scratch and dig, wanting the object to fall free so we could see what it was.

It took some doing. The object was firmly embedded. Martha helped. It turned out to be a bone. We were shocked because it looked a lot like a human bone. "It's human, I know it is," Esteban said. "Let's dig more and see if we can find the rest of it."

We dug and dug, scratching with our fingers and with sticks. We hid the bone when it was time to go home, and we went back the next day with shovels. In the end we found a skull, most of a human rib cage, and many bits and pieces of what had once been a living human being.

It scared me to be digging and finding human bones. I could not help but continue. It was too mysterious and strange to be ignored. Besides, when Esteban told me not to be "chicken," I had no choice but to stay and help dig.

Martha got scared. She stopped digging and went home. A part of me wanted to go with her. It was my love of Esteban that kept me there.

Once we had all the bones out of the bank, we needed a place to hide them. "That culvert nobody uses anymore," Esteban said. "That's a good hiding place." Only black widow spiders, and maybe a snake or two, ever used the culvert. It was perfect.

For a week we went to visit the bones each day. More than once we took them out of the culvert and handled them. We wondered out loud to each other whose bones they were. I expressed a fear about touching someone's bones. Esteban said, "Don't be such a baby. You're nothing but a kid."

One afternoon a brilliant thought came into my mind. "These are the remains of an ancient one," I said. I whispered the words because I was impressed with my discovery.

"How so?" said Esteban.

"There are kinds of scientists who dig up old bones, really old ones, thousands and thousands of years old. They take the bones to museums. I bet this is one of those thousands-of-years-old people." The thought soothed me, so much that I smiled. It was possible we were not doing evil at all. We were being archaeologists.

Two weeks passed, with regular visits to the bones. My guilt came back and got the better of me. I decided to go to the culvert on my own, collect the bones, and bury them. I would face

Esteban, and his scorn, when the time came. Meanwhile, I was sure burial was the right thing to do.

When I got to the place where we'd hidden the bones, there was nothing to be seen, not a scrap, not the smallest white bit.

As soon as I could, I confronted Esteban. "What did you do with them?" I asked. "You must have done something. You're the only other person who knows the bones exist."

"So what if I took them?" Esteban replied. "They belong to me as much as to you."

"You might have told me before you took them," I said, feeling betrayed.

"Why should I tell you anything? It's none of your business."

"If you're my friend, then you tell me things," I said, dismayed by what he was saying. "Friends tell each other things."

Esteban turned his handsome face in my direction. His eyes were glowing with a fire of pleasure I had never seen before. "Look, you idiot, you girl. You must be crazy to think I could be your friend. You're white. You're female. Your father is a racist, right? How can you think we'd be friends?"

I had never seen Esteban behave this way. This was a person I did not know. I wanted to kill him, to pound him, and I wanted to cry, all at once. "You're horrible!" I screamed. Tears came. I could not stop them. "I hate you!"

"Hate is what your father is best at," Esteban told me. "Your father is a pro at hating people."

When Esteban said these words, I felt as if my head were being run over by a truck. I let him go when he ran off. He didn't care about me at all. He despised me.

I was sure my father would banish me from the house forever and never allow me back. He was that angry when he heard about the bones.

It turned out Esteban had sold the bones to his older brothers for money. Then, when Esteban's father found out what was going on, he came to our house. He blamed everything on me. "Your little girl?" Mr. Gabaldon said in a fury. "Your little girl is a grave robber. She goes around desecrating graves. She is evil."

"He's lying. He's wrong," I cried desperately. "I promise you, he's wrong. It never happened that way."

My father stood before me, his face red, his eyes filled with disgust. I pictured him exploding. There would be fragments of him all over the room, clinging to the walls and sticking to the furniture.

"Let her speak, dear," my mother said. She came into the room so quietly that we didn't know she was there until she spoke. "Let her tell her story. Jenny doesn't lie."

I told the whole of it, even confessing I'd fallen in love with Esteban. I said I'd been betrayed. When I was finished, I was worn out. I didn't care anymore if I got banished. Death would be fine, too.

My parents believed me. I had to go over the story a few times, but in the end my mother and father nodded their heads and accepted that I was telling them the truth.

Esteban's name never passed my lips again. When we had to stand at the bus stop together, we ignored each other.

Later on I found out the bones belonged to someone who had died a long time before, perhaps forty years past. The person's family could not afford a town burial, and so they chose a spot by the river as a grave. Flash floods had washed the riverbank away, and after so many years the bones were finally revealed. They were reburied in the yard behind the church, on high ground, well away from the river.

Alone with My Father

My grandfather, my mother's father, was alone and ill in Chicago. My two uncles called and told my mother to come. "He may be dying," they told her. "It may be the last time you see him."

My mother went, and she took the twins with her. "It may be a sad occasion for them," she said at dinner the night before going. "But they'll see a little of the city."

My mother was from Chicago. She clearly missed being there. I knew this from the stories she told about her life in Chicago before any of us were born.

"All my girls will see the city someday," she said. "Even you, Jenny dear."

My mother was forgetting that I'd already seen the city once and hated it. As a family we'd taken a trip to Chicago, and all I could think of the whole time was getting back home. The twins were happy they were going, and I was glad to be left behind.

"Hug Grandpa for me," I said as my mother and sisters prepared to board the train that would take them away. "Tell him how much I love him, okay?"

"Of course, dear. Now you be good," my mother said. She squeezed my hand, kissed my father on the cheek, and they were gone.

I was nearly twelve when my mother took the twins to Chicago. It would be my first time alone with my father. Many times he had gone off and left us with my mother. This time the tables were turned.

"We'll do things together," he told me. We were driving back to the ranch from the train station. "We'll have fun together, you'll see."

We had not done much together in my life so far. I did not know what to expect.

Three days after my mother's departure, I came in to supper and saw my father sitting at the kitchen table, a bottle of whiskey at his elbow. He was drunk.

Edna was at the sink, her back to him. Bill was down at the barn, finishing evening chores.

I settled into my usual chair, not knowing what to make of it.

"Listen up," my father said. His speech was slurred. He stared at me, and I stiffened. "We're going to make a decision about that pig, the one you call Jerome."

My heart pounded. What could he mean?

"He broke into the orchard again."

I knew Jerome had a bad habit of breaking down his plank fence and going after windfalls in the orchard. Although he was a full-grown boar, Jerome was gentle. He came when he was called.

"You just need to call him and he'll come," I said. "I'll fix the fence tomorrow morning, I promise."

"I don't need to do anything of the kind," my father said. "The decision is made. I'm calling Stanley in the morning. The pig will be butchered, soon as I can get Stanley over here."

So, it was happening. Stanley was the valley murderer, at least that's what I called him. Stanley was the man who, with his gun, hired himself out to kill animals at butchering time. He was known for his direct shots to the brain.

"You shouldn't be drinking in front of your girl," Edna said. "It isn't right that she see you this way. You wouldn't be talking like this about Jerome if you were sober."

"That's enough from you, Edna," my father said. He took a swig from the bottle and slammed it down hard on the wooden table. "This is none of your damn business."

Bill came into the room. He took his place at the table, his eyes darting from me, to Edna, to my father, and then back to me. "What's with the drinking?" he asked. "Why the bottle after all this time?"

Silence.

"You're drunk," Bill said.

"So what if I am?"

"It's wrong, dead wrong," Edna said.

"He told me he's going to call Stanley in the morning and have Jerome shot," I said to Bill.

"You have no right to do that without checking with me," Bill said. "No right. Those hogs are my responsibility."

"He wouldn't talk this way if he were sober," Edna said again.

"Be quiet, all of you. Stop this jabbering." My father's face twisted into a grimace, as if his stomach hurt. He took another drink from the bottle. "My mind is made up. That pig is a waste of time. Never did make a mark at the State Fair. Not even last prize. I'm sick and tired of fixing the fence. He goes, and that's that."

We all fell into a silence that lasted for several minutes. The room was warm, but I felt cold. After a while it was Bill who spoke. "Just because

Emmy is away is no reason to start drinking."

"She wouldn't like seeing you this way," Edna said.

"I do as I please. My wife has nothing to say about what I do or don't do. A man's life is his own."

An even longer silence came. My father continued to take gulps from the bottle, which was nearing the half-empty mark. In my mind I had already given up. My father's word, sober or drunk, was the final one. We all knew that.

"Call Stanley in the morning, first thing. Get him over here early. That's an order, Bill."

I ran from the room. Edna came to talk to me before I went to bed that night. She brought some food, leftovers from supper.

"I can't eat," I told her.

"Your father has a drinking problem," Edna said, putting the plate of food down. "He's had one as long as we've known him. He just doesn't usually get like this. At least, he hasn't for a lot of years."

"I don't care about him," I said. "It's Jerome I care about."

"There are things we can't change, no matter how much we want to or how hard we try."

"Maybe."

"You knew this would come someday, from the moment Jerome was born, didn't you?"

"Yes, that's true. I just didn't think it would happen this way."

"I know," Edna said, hugging me tight. "I know."

I was up before dawn and down at the sheds. I would let Jerome loose. He would run off into the hills and make a life for himself. He would become a feral pig, a domestic pig gone wild.

Bill anticipated my move. He was waiting for me by Jerome's pen.

"Let me let him go, please, Bill?"

"You can't rightly do that," Bill said. "It's your father's call this time."

"He can't decide things when he's drunk."

"I haven't called Stanley yet," Bill said. "I won't until I have some words with your father. Give it some time, kid. Wait on it."

I promised I would.

At noon that day, Stanley's truck rolled to a

stop by the gate to the lower pasture.

My father walked through the field to the sheds to meet Stanley and supervise the slaughter. His features were puffy from drinking most of the night. He staggered, but he didn't fall.

Stanley unlatched the gate and headed for the sheds. He carried a rifle, loaded and ready. Stanley brought his wife along. She did the skinning out. I watched them both come near to where I stood. Stanley's wife was skinny. Her bleached curls were tight against her skull.

Something in me snapped. I lost control.

"You can't do this!" I screamed, hurling myself at Stanley. "You can't kill my pig!"

"Get this brat off me," Stanley yelled.

"I won't let you kill my pig!" I screamed again.

Stanley and his wife both stepped backward, trying to get away from me. "What's with this kid," Stanley said. "She crazy or something?"

Bill had come running. He stepped between Stanley and me, saying, "She's not crazy. It's her pig."

Bill led me away by the arm. I let him. When

I heard the shot, I turned and watched Jerome fall. The noonday sun shone on his belly.

I never went near that spot in the pasture, the exact place where Jerome died. To me it was ground that would always be like a battlefield when the war is over—too painful to stand on.

The Tree House

In a lot of ways my childhood ended the day the bullet went into Jerome's brain and killed him. From what happened, I learned how some things have to end, while life goes on pretty much as it did before.

My father drank for another day, and then he got into the truck and drove away. Edna said,

"He's probably going to Indian country. That's what he does when he's hurting."

"He has a hole in his middle," Bill told me. "It's a wound you can't see. People like him suffer from the harm they do, but they go right on doing it."

My mother and sisters came home, but nobody talked to me about the pig's death. The truth was inside me forever. I suppose all of us knew talking about it wouldn't change anything.

The only person I ever mentioned Jerome's name to was Bill. "Stella said something once. About Jerome's bringing sadness to me. I wonder how she knew."

"Hard to say," Bill answered. "Except that Stella knows things other people don't."

My mother wanted my father to fix things up between us. She wanted us to smooth it over. "Your father loves you, dear," she said to me. "He's sorry for what he did. Remember, he loves you."

The words about love were familiar because I'd heard them all my life, every time my father did something to make one of us sad. My mother always insisted that under the surface, in his heart, my father felt love for us, his children.

"You've always wanted a tree house, right?"

My father asked me this about a month after Jerome died.

"Yes," I said. "I have."

"Then lets build one together," he said.

We picked out lumber from a pile in back of the barn. I got nails and a hammer. "Get two hammers," my father told me. "I'm helping you build this thing."

I went back and got another hammer and more nails.

We chose a silver poplar by the river, on the north edge of the ranch property. The tree was one of a big grove that stood at the top end of a pasture. Indians owned the land. They grazed ponies on the pasture grass.

My father was big and bulky. He wasn't used to climbing trees. He smashed his fingers a few times with the hammer. This made him swear, but he kept on working.

We made steps and nailed them into place. We hammered the floorboards together with braces and lifted the whole piece into the tree. After the floor was in position, we built the walls. It was a three-sided house, with no windows.

Martha stayed around to watch us work. She didn't want to climb the tree, so she looked up at us from below. Junior came around, too. Since he couldn't climb trees, he remained on the ground next to Martha.

I began to like the idea of a tree house as it took shape and form. It would be mine, and mine alone. I would share it with my friends and Kim. Anyone else wanting to come in would have to ask for permission.

The last thing we did was nail some scraps of tin to the roof so the house would stay dry when it rained or snowed. After it was finished, I decided to have a celebration, a housewarming.

Martha climbed into the tree house with no trouble. Getting Junior in was a bigger problem.

I pulled from above and Martha pushed from below. We finally got Junior up, with him wondering all the while how many of his bones would get broken if he fell.

Bill, who was smart about ropes, helped us

rig a system so that we could raise and lower Junior without risking any broken limbs. The three of us spent a lot of happy hours in that tree house. It was a refuge, a sanctuary, and a place we could go for time out from the rest of the world.

My father knew he could come to the tree house anytime he wanted. He never did. Kim liked it, but Tasha said it was "kid stuff" and "silly." My mother came to admire it and take some pictures with her camera, but she never climbed the tree.

My mother's desire to see things patched up between my father and me was mostly realized. Outwardly, at least, there was nothing much different about the way he behaved with me. In my heart, however, there was a change. I felt afraid of him. I knew I would always have that fear inside me.